Alfie Gives a Hand

Other Picture Books by
SHIRLEY HUGHES

Alfie's Feet

Alfie Gets in First

Dogger
(Winner of the 1977 Kate Greenaway Medal)

An Evening at Alfie's

Helpers
*(Highly commended for the 1975 Kate Greenaway
Medal and winner of the 1976 Other Award)*

Moving Molly

Sally's Secret

The Trouble with Jack

Up and Up

British Library Cataloguing in Publication Data
Hughes, Shirley   Alfie gives a hand.
I. Title   823'.914 [J]   PZ7   ISBN 0-370-30521-3
Copyright © Shirley Hughes 1983   Printed and bound in Great Britain for
The Bodley Head Ltd, 30 Bedford Square, London WC1B 3RP
by W. S. Cowell Ltd, Ipswich
First published 1983   Reprinted 1985

Alfie Gives a Hand

Shirley Hughes

THE BODLEY HEAD

London

One day Alfie came home from Nursery School with a card in an envelope. His best friend, Bernard, had given it to him.

"Look, it's got my name on it," said
Alfie, pointing.

Mum said that it was an invitation to
Bernard's birthday tea party.

"Will it be at Bernard's house?" Alfie wanted to know. He'd never been there before. Mum said yes, and she told him all about birthday parties, and how you had to take a present, and about the games and how there would be nice things to eat.

Alfie was very excited about Bernard's party. When the day came Mum washed Alfie's face and brushed his hair and helped him put on a clean T-shirt and his brand-new shorts.

"You and Annie Rose are going to be at the party, too, aren't you?" asked Alfie.

"Oh, no," said Mum. "I'll take you to Bernard's house and then Annie Rose and I will go to the park and come back to collect you when it's time to go home."

"But I want you to be there," said Alfie.

Mum told him that she and Annie Rose hadn't been invited to the party, only Alfie, because he was Bernard's special friend.

"You don't mind my leaving you at Nursery School, do you?" she said. "So you won't mind being at Bernard's house either, as soon as you get there."

Mum had bought some crayons for Alfie to give Bernard for his birthday present. While she was wrapping them up, Alfie went upstairs. He looked under his pillow and found his old bit of blanket which he kept in bed with him at night.

He brought it downstairs, and sat down to wait for Mum.

"You won't want your old blanket at the party," said Mum, when it was time to go.

But Alfie wouldn't leave his blanket behind. He held it tightly with one hand, and Bernard's present with the other, all the way to Bernard's house.

When they got there, Bernard's Mum opened the door.
"Hello, Alfie," she said. "Let's go into the garden
and find Bernard and the others."
Then Mum gave Alfie a kiss and said good-bye,
and went off to the park with Annie Rose.

"Would you like to put your blanket down here with the coats?" asked Bernard's Mum. But Alfie didn't want to put his blanket down. He still held on to it very tightly.

Bernard was in the garden with Min and Sam and Daniel and some other children from the Nursery School.

"Happy birthday!" Alfie remembered to say, and he gave Bernard his present. Bernard pulled off the paper.

"Crayons! How lovely!" said Bernard's Mum. "Say thank you, Bernard."

"Thank you," said Bernard. But do you know what he did then?

He threw the crayons up in the air. They landed all
over the grass.

"That was a silly thing to do," said Bernard's Mum,
as she picked up the crayons and put them away.

Then Bernard's Mum brought out some bubble stuff and blew lots of bubbles into the air. They floated all over the garden and the children jumped about trying to pop them.

Alfie couldn't pop many bubbles because he was holding on to his blanket. But Bernard jumped about and pushed and popped more bubbles than anyone else.

"Don't push people, Bernard," said Bernard's Mum sternly.

One huge bubble landed lightly on Min's sleeve. It stayed there, quivering and shiny. Min smiled. She stood very still.

Then Bernard came up
behind her and popped
the big bubble.

Min began to cry.
Bernard's Mum was
cross with Bernard and
told him to say he
was sorry.

"Never mind, we're going to have tea now, dear," she told
Min. "Who would you like to sit next to?"

Min wanted to sit next to Alfie. She stopped crying and
pulled her chair right up close to his.

For tea there were sandwiches and little sausages on sticks and crisps and jellies and a big iced cake with candles and "Happy Birthday, Bernard" written on it.

Bernard took a huge breath and blew out
all the candles at once – *Phoooooo!* Everyone
clapped and sang "Happy Birthday to You".

Then Bernard blew into his lemonade through his straw and made rude bubbling noises. He blew into his jelly, too, until his Mum took it away from him.

Alfie liked the tea . . . but holding on to his blanket made eating rather difficult. It got all mixed up with the jelly and crisps, and covered in sticky crumbs.

After tea, Bernard's Mum said that they were all going to play a game. But Bernard ran off and fetched his very best present. It was a tiger mask.

Bernard went behind a bush and came out wearing the mask and making terrible growling noises: "Grrr! Grrr, grrrr, GRRRR! ACHT!"

He went crawling round the garden,
sounding very fierce and frightening.

Min began to cry again. She clung on to
Alfie.

"Get up *at once*, Bernard," said Bernard's Mum. "It's not that kind of game. Now let's all stand in a circle, everyone, and join hands."

Bernard stopped growling, but he wouldn't take off his tiger mask. Instead he grabbed Alfie's hand to pull him into the circle.

Bernard's Mum tried to take Min's hand and bring her into the circle, too. But Min wouldn't hold anyone's hand but Alfie's. She went on crying. She cried and cried.

Then Alfie made a brave decision. He ran and put down his blanket, very carefully, in a safe place underneath the table.

Now he could hold Min's hand, too, as well as Bernard's.

Min stopped crying. She wasn't frightened of Bernard in his tiger mask now she was holding Alfie's hand.

She joined in the game and they all
danced round together, singing:

"Ring-a-ring-o'-roses
A pocket full of posies
A-tishoo, a-tishoo,
We all fall DOWN!"

Afterwards Alfie and Min joined in with
some more games and ate ice-cream and
pop-corn and bounced balloons with the
others. Alfie had such a good time that his
blanket stayed under the table until Mum
and Annie Rose came to collect him.

"What a helpful guest you've been, Alfie," said Bernard's Mum, when Alfie thanked her and said good-bye. "Min wouldn't have enjoyed the party a bit without you. I *do* wish Bernard would learn to be helpful sometimes –

– Perhaps he will, one day."

On the way home, Alfie carried his
blanket in one hand and a balloon and a
packet of sweets in the other. His blanket
had got a bit messy at the party. It had been
rather in the way, too. Next time he thought
he might leave it safely at home, after all.